THIS BOOK BELONGS TO...

Name:

Age:

Favourite player:

2024/25

My Predictions   **Actual**

The Hornets' final position:

The Hornets' top scorer:

Championship winners:

Championship top scorer:

FA Cup winners:

EFL Cup winners:

Contributors: Andy Greeves, Kevin Newman, Seth Nobes, Dan Palmer, Peter Rogers, Steve Scott, Archie Smith.

A TWOCAN PUBLICATION

©2024. Published by twocan under licence from Watford Football Club.

Every effort has been made to ensure the accuracy of information within this publication but the publishers cannot be held responsible for any errors or omissions. Views expressed are those of the authors and do not necessarily represent those of the publishers or the football club. All rights reserved.

978-1-916755-08-6   £11

PICTURE CREDITS: Alamy, Alan Cozzi.

CONTENTS

Championship Squad 2024/25	06
Footy Drills - Fitness First	22
Ryan Porteous Poster	23
Meet Your Rivals	24
Watford Women	28
Total Legend - Luther Blissett	30
Spot the Season	31
Wordsearch	32
Moussa Sissoko Poster	33
Danger Men	34
Tom Dele-Bashiru Poster	38
Spot the Season	39
Player of the Season	40
Footy Drills - Attack Attack	42
Yasser Larouci Poster	43
Vakoun Bayo Poster	44
Snap Shot	45
The Big Match - Goalscorers	46
Total Legend - Helen Ward	47
Fact or Fib?	48
Goal of the Season	50
Total Legend - John Barnes	52
The Big Match - Appearances	53
Jeremy Ngakia Poster	54
Complete the Badge	55
Spot the Season	56
Tom Ince Poster	57
Footy Drills - Shot Stopping	58
Total Legend - Troy Deeney	59
Francisco Sierralta Poster	60
Spot the Season	61
Quiz and Puzzle Answers	62

JEREMY NGAKIA

2

| POSITION: | Defender | COUNTRY: | England | DOB: | 07/09/2000 |

Jeremy Ngakia burst onto the Premier League scene in 2020 before joining Watford the following summer from West Ham. The full-back featured in both a promotion-winning campaign and a Premier League season before helping the Hornets to a mid-table Championship finish in 2022/23. He played 15 times throughout 2023/24 in a campaign hit by injury.

FRANCISCO SIERRALTA

3

| POSITION: | Defender | COUNTRY: | Chile | DOB: | 06/05/1997 |

Signing in 2020 from sister club Udinese, Sierralta had to wait patiently to make his senior debut for the Hornets. The Chilean almost won the fans' player of the year prize in the 2020/21 promotion-winning campaign and has continued to provide strength and a dominant aerial ability at the back for the Golden Boys, featuring 31 times last term.

KÉVIN KEBEN — 4

POSITION: Defender **COUNTRY:** Cameroon **DOB:** 26/01/2004

Watford FC confirmed the signing of centre-back Kévin Keben from Ligue 1 side Toulouse on a four-year deal in August 2024. The Cameroonian made eight appearances in the French top-flight last season, as well as two more in the UEFA Europa League. He is an Under-23 international for his country and featured 21 times in all for Toulouse.

RYAN PORTEOUS — 5

POSITION: Defender **COUNTRY:** Scotland **DOB:** 25/03/1999

Centre back Ryan Porteous joined Watford on a four-and-a-half-year deal from Hibernian in January 2023. The Scot netted a debut goal for the Hornets and instantly won the approval of fans by always fighting for the cause. Alongside his defensive qualities, Porteous also has offensive prowess and made 47 appearances for club and country last term.

THE CHAMPIONSHIP SQUAD 24/25

WATFORD

MATTIE POLLOCK

6

POSITION: Defender **COUNTRY:** England **DOB:** 28/09/2001

Defender Mattie Pollock signed for Watford in May 2021 before having spells on loan at Cheltenham Town and Aberdeen. The warrior at the back worked his way into the first team, eventually making his first starting appearance of last season in January 2024. Pollock lasted the whole 90 minutes in Watford's first clean sheet in almost three months, showing his rapid development in a Hornets shirt.

THE CHAMPIONSHIP SQUAD 24/25

TOM INCE — 7
POSITION: Midfielder **COUNTRY:** England **DOB:** 30/01/1992

Tom Ince signed for the Golden Boys on a two-year deal in June 2023 following Reading's relegation. Returning to the second tier, Ince featured 29 times for Watford, in both the Championship and the FA Cup. The winger made his mark early on with his curling effort against West Brom which was a contender for the club's goal of the season.

GIORGI CHAKVETADZE — 8
POSITION: Midfielder **COUNTRY:** Georgia **DOB:** 29/08/1999

Giorgi Chakvetadze was a shining light for the Hornets in 2023/24. The creative midfielder initially starred on a season long loan from KAA Gent before the club made the move permanent in January 2024. Alongside scoring his first goal on Boxing Day, the Georgian's flair, dribbling and performances for his country won the appreciation of many fans.

IMRÂN LOUZA

10

POSITION: Midfielder **COUNTRY:** Morocco **DOB:** 01/05/1999

Moroccan Imrân Louza was the club's most expensive signing in the summer transfer window of 2021/22. Signing from Nantes, the midfielder has been appreciated by Watford fans for his vision and ball control, as shown when making a positive impression in both the Premier League and Championship. Louza scored with a well-executed finish in the 4-0 victory over QPR on the first day of the 2023/24 season.

ROCCO VATA

POSITION: Forward **COUNTRY:** Ireland **DOB:** 18/04/2005

Winger Rocco Vata joined the Hornets before the 2024/25 season after he parted ways with his boyhood club Celtic. Vata caught the eye last term, training with the Bhoys' senior squad and scoring 13 times for the B-team. Vata has shown his potential in a Watford shirt, demonstrating his ability to weave his way past defenders and create chances in the final third.

KEN SEMA

POSITION: Midfielder **COUNTRY:** Sweden **DOB:** 30/09/1993

Signing from Östersunds FK in 2018, the Swede boasted a winning goal against Arsenal before signing for the Golden Boys. Making his debut for the Hornets against Brighton in 2018, King Ken instantly became a popular figure for Watford fans and a regular feature in the first-team. He appeared 32 times last term, scoring in the Yellows' first away win in 11 months against Swansea.

THE CHAMPIONSHIP SQUAD 24/25

KAYKY ALMEIDA — 13

POSITION: Defender **COUNTRY:** Brazil **DOB:** 01/05/2005

Kayky Almeida joined Watford in August 2024 from Brazilian top-flight outfit Fluminense, on a deal which will retain his services until 2029. The left-footed defender made his senior professional debut for his former club with a substitute appearance. Hornets Head Coach Tom Cleverley has tipped the South American as one for the future.

PIERRE DWOMOH — 14

POSITION: Midfielder **COUNTRY:** Belgium **DOB:** 21/06/2004

Pierre Dwomoh joined the Hornets in August 2024 from Antwerp in his native Belgium. The midfielder is a youth international for his country who has also played for Genk. He is considered an exciting prospect for the future at Vicarage Road.

THE CHAMPIONSHIP SQUAD 24/25

ANTONIO TIKVIĆ — 15

POSITION: Defender **COUNTRY:** Croatia **DOB:** 21/04/2004

Former Bayern Munich reserve player Antonio Tikvić joined the Hornets on a season-long loan from sister club Udinese in the summer of 2024. The Croatian ball-playing defender will compete for a place in the Watford backline and has already made Serie A and Coppa Italia appearances for Udinese.

MOUSSA SISSOKO — 17

POSITION: Midfielder **COUNTRY:** France **DOB:** 16/08/1989

Former Tottenham star Sissoko re-signed for Watford in July 2024 on a two-year-deal. In his earlier years at Toulouse, the Frenchman played alongside future Hornet Etienne Capoue and, in 2019, he featured in a Champions League final for Spurs. The Frenchman was a regular captain for Watford throughout the 2021/22 Premier League campaign before moving to Nantes. The dynamic midfielder brings a wealth of experience on his return to the Golden Boys this season.

DANIEL JEBBISON — 18

POSITION: Forward **COUNTRY:** England **DOB:** 13/08/2003

England youth international Daniel Jebbison signed for the Hornets on a season-long loan from AFC Bournemouth in August 2024. The former Sheffield United man is an England Under-21 international and won the UEFA Under-19 Championship in 2022. When scoring for the Blades against Everton in 2021, he became the youngest player to ever net on their first Premier League start.

VAKOUN BAYO — 19

POSITION: Forward **COUNTRY:** Ivory Coast **DOB:** 10/01/1997

Vakoun Bayo joined Watford in July 2022 from RSC Charleroi. Having been potent in front of goal in Belgium, the Ivorian scored an important winner against Middlesborough on The Vic 100 matchday before returning to Charleroi on loan for the remainder of the season. Last term, Bayo's hard-work and pressing ability won the appreciation of many fans, and he also netted seven times in 42 appearances. He joined Udinese in August 2024 but was loaned straight back.

MAMADOU DOUMBIA

20

POSITION: Forward   **COUNTRY:** Mali   **DOB:** 18/02/2006

Left-footed front-man Mamadou Doumbia signed for the Hornets on a five-year-contract in February 2024 before linking-up with his team-mates at London Colney in July. Impressive performances for Malian side Black Stars FC and internationally for the Malian Under-17s showcased his attacking flair, hold up play and finishing, and earned him a place in the Hornets' squad for the 2024/25 season.

THE CHAMPIONSHIP SQUAD 24/25

ANGELO OGBONNA — 21
POSITION: Defender **COUNTRY:** Italy **DOB:** 23/05/1998

Experienced central defender Angelo Ogbonna joined the Hornets in August 2024 after he departed West Ham. He made 17 appearances in all competitions in 2023/24, including seven starts in the Premier League. Ogbonna was also part of the West Ham side that won the UEFA Europa Conference League in 2023, while the former Juventus man played at Euro 2012 and Euro 2016 for his country.

JAMES MORRIS — 22
POSITION: Defender **COUNTRY:** England **DOB:** 23/11/2001

A solid showing as a trialist in a 2021 pre-season fixture against West Brom earned James Morris a move to Watford. Originally linking up with the Under-21 squad, he made his professional debut in the FA Cup against Leicester in January 2023 and signed a new three-year-deal that April. The left-back's minutes on the pitch continued to rise during the 2023/24 season, where he featured 16 times.

THE CHAMPIONSHIP SQUAD 24/25

JONATHAN BOND — **23**

POSITION: **Goalkeeper** COUNTRY: **England** DOB: **19/05/1993**

Jonathan Bond returned to Vicarage Road in July 2024. The keeper had previously been involved in the academy set-up from the age of 10, and was part of the side that gained promotion to the Premier League in the 2014/15 season. Bond will provide competition for the number one jersey at the Hornets.

TOM DELE-BASHIRU — **24**

POSITION: **Midfielder** COUNTRY: **Nigeria** DOB: **17/09/1999**

Tom Dele-Bashiru arrived at the Hornets in 2019 after departing Manchester City. After making a positive impression on loan at Reading, the midfielder thrived in Watford's team throughout 2023/24, where he displayed his close control and dribbling. In his breakout season, Dele-Bashiru netted on the first day of the campaign within 33 seconds against QPR.

KWADWO BAAH

34

POSITION: Forward **COUNTRY:** Germany **DOB:** 27/01/2003

Having made his senior debut for Rochdale at the age of 16, Kwadwo Baah was confirmed as a promising talent in the EFL. He joined Watford in 2021 and spent time out on loan in Germany and League One. Having now returned to the Hornets, he looks set to kick-on and make an impact in the 2024/25 season.

FESTY EBOSELE — 36

POSITION: Defender **COUNTRY:** Ireland **DOB:** 02/08/2002

Festy Ebosele joined the Hornets on a season-long loan from Udinese in August 2024. The Republic of Ireland international is a right-sided player who adds to Head Coach Tom Cleverley's wing-back options ahead of the 2024/25 campaign. Ebosele played for Derby County before moving to the Serie A club in 2022.

YASSER LAROUCI — 37

POSITION: Defender **COUNTRY:** Algeria **DOB:** 01/01/2001

With a year of Premier League experience to his name with Sheffield United, Yasser Larouci signed on a season-long loan in August from Troyes in France. The versatile defender played a part in Algeria's campaign at the 2023 Africa Cup of Nations and represented quality on the left in 47 appearances for Troyes. Larouci is an attacking wing-back who is set to provide a threat with his pace and crossing on the flanks.

THE CHAMPIONSHIP SQUAD 24/25

EDO KAYEMBE — 39
POSITION: Midfielder **COUNTRY:** DR Congo **DOB:** 03/06/1998

DR Congo international Edo Kayembe joined Watford in 2022 from Eupen. Making 13 appearances in the top-flight during his first season with the Hornets, the midfielder gained the reputation of being a box-to-box player and featured in both the 2022/23 and 2023/24 campaigns. Last term, Kayembe showed his attacking credentials with five goals.

RYAN ANDREWS — 45
POSITION: Defender **COUNTRY:** England **DOB:** 26/08/2004

England Under-20 international and youth graduate Ryan Andrews became an important player for the Hornets during 2023/24. The right-back featured 44 times and notched three goals and two assists. Andrews likes to shoot from range while making overlapping runs down the right-flank. He scored some notable goals, including his first senior strike against Birmingham City in September 2023.

YOU WILL NEED CONES OR MARKERS, A BALL AND A FRIEND!

SHUTTLE RUNS AREA GREAT FITNESS TRAINING EXERCISE TO HELP BUILD SPEED, STAMINA, ACCELERATION AND ENDURANCE.

FOOTY DRILLS
FITNESS FIRST

EASY
Set up a line of 6-8 cones 5 metres apart. To begin with, run from the first cone to the second cone and back again. Next, run to the second cone and back again. Continue to do this until you have completed a run to the final cone.

HARD
Now, add a football into the mix! Dribble from the start to the first cone, turn with the ball, pass back to your friend and then sprint back to the start. Your friend should stop the ball at the start where you will gain possession and dribble to the second cone. Repeat this process for each of the cones.

EXPERT
There are many ways you can increase the difficulty level of this drill. Have your friend throw the ball to you as you're running back to the start. You will have to work to bring the ball under control, bring it back to the start and dribble on to the next cone - work on chest traps, thigh traps or traps with the feet.

Adding a football helps players control the ball at top speeds and when the body is tired.

Remember to swap roles with your friend so you both get a chance to work on your fitness!

As you improve, try and work faster. Try inventing some of your own ways to make this drill harder?

START

It's time to get to grips with the Championship and...
MEET YOUR RIVALS

BLACKBURN ROVERS
GROUND: Ewood Park **CAPACITY:** 31,363
MANAGER: John Eustace **NICKNAME:** Rovers
2023/24 LEAGUE POSITION: 19th
DID YOU KNOW:
Rovers were Premier League Champions in 1994/95.

CARDIFF CITY
GROUND: Cardiff City Stadium **CAPACITY:** 33,280
MANAGER: Erol Bulut **NICKNAME:** The Bluebirds
2023/24 LEAGUE POSITION: 12th
DID YOU KNOW:
Current Wales manager Craig Bellamy was born in Cardiff and ended his playing career with a spell at the Bluebirds.

BRISTOL CITY
GROUND: Ashton Gate **CAPACITY:** 26,459
MANAGER: Liam Manning **NICKNAME:** The Robins
2023/24 LEAGUE POSITION: 11th
DID YOU KNOW:
Bristol City last competed in the top division of English football in 1979/80.

COVENTRY CITY
GROUND: Coventry Building Society Arena
CAPACITY: 32,609
MANAGER: Mark Robins **NICKNAME:** Sky Blues
2023/24 LEAGUE POSITION: 9th
DID YOU KNOW:
Since leaving their former home at Highfield Road in 2005, the Sky Blues have played home games at four different grounds.

BURNLEY
GROUND: Turf Moor **CAPACITY:** 21,744
MANAGER: Scott Parker **NICKNAME:** The Clarets
2023/24 LEAGUE POSITION: 19th Premier League
DID YOU KNOW:
Burnley boss Scott Parker has previously won promotion from the Championship with two different teams.

DERBY COUNTY
GROUND: Pride Park **CAPACITY:** 32,956
MANAGER: Paul Warne **NICKNAME:** The Rams
2023/24 LEAGUE POSITION: 2nd League One
DID YOU KNOW:
Curtis Nelson was the only player to start all 46 games of the Rams' 23/24 promotion-winning season.

HULL CITY

GROUND: MKM Stadium **CAPACITY:** 24,983
MANAGER: Tim Walter **NICKNAME:** The Tigers
2023/24 LEAGUE POSITION: 7th

DID YOU KNOW:
Hull City had never played top-flight football until they won promotion to the Premier League in 2008.

MIDDLESBROUGH

GROUND: Riverside Stadium **CAPACITY:** 33,931
MANAGER: Michael Carrick **NICKNAME:** Boro
2023/24 LEAGUE POSITION: 8th

DID YOU KNOW:
Striker Emmanuel Latte Lath enjoyed an impressive end to 2023/24 with eleven goals in the final three months of the season.

LEEDS UNITED

GROUND: Elland Road **CAPACITY:** 37,608
MANAGER: Daniel Farke **NICKNAME:** The Whites
2023/24 LEAGUE POSITION: 3rd

DID YOU KNOW:
Prior to the formation of the Premier League in 1992/93, Leeds United were the last team to win the old First Division title when they were crowned champions in 1991/92.

MILLWALL

GROUND: The Den **CAPACITY:** 19,369
MANAGER: Neil Harris **NICKNAME:** The Lions
2023/24 LEAGUE POSITION: 13th

DID YOU KNOW:
Lions boss Neil Harris is also the club's record league goalscorer having netted 124 league goals during his playing days at The Den.

LUTON TOWN

GROUND: Kenilworth Road **CAPACITY:** 12,056
MANAGER: Rob Edwards **NICKNAME:** The Hatters
2023/24 LEAGUE POSITION: 18th Premier League

DID YOU KNOW:
In the 1980s Luton Town were one of four clubs to install plastic pitches.

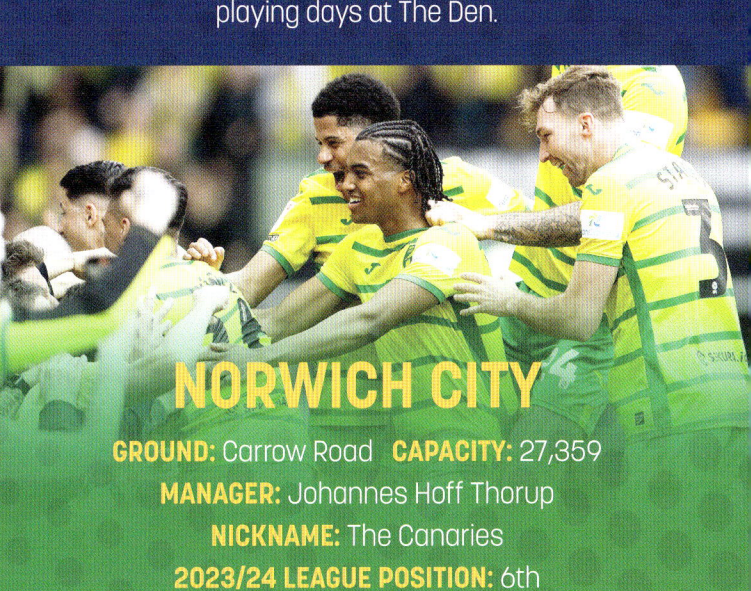

NORWICH CITY

GROUND: Carrow Road **CAPACITY:** 27,359
MANAGER: Johannes Hoff Thorup
NICKNAME: The Canaries
2023/24 LEAGUE POSITION: 6th

DID YOU KNOW:
Norwich City boast a proud record in East Anglian derby matches against arch-rivals Ipswich Town and remain unbeaten against Town in 15 years.

It's time to get to grips with the Championship and...

MEET YOUR RIVALS

OXFORD UNITED
GROUND: Kassam Stadium **CAPACITY:** 12,537
MANAGER: Des Buckingham **NICKNAME:** The U's
2023/24 LEAGUE POSITION: 5th League One
DID YOU KNOW:
The 2024/25 season will see Oxford's Kassam Stadium as the only three-sided ground in the Championship.

PRESTON NORTH END
GROUND: Deepdale **CAPACITY:** 23,404
MANAGER: Paul Heckingbottom **NICKNAME:** North End
2023/24 LEAGUE POSITION: 10th
DID YOU KNOW:
Deepdale has been Preston North End's only home ground, the club have hosted matches there since 1881.

PLYMOUTH ARGYLE
GROUND: Home Park **CAPACITY:** 17,000
MANAGER: Wayne Rooney **NICKNAME:** The Pilgrims
2023/24 LEAGUE POSITION: 21st
DID YOU KNOW:
Plymouth fans will face a 667-mile round trip from Home Park to Sunderland's Stadium of Light when the two clubs meet in 2024/25 with the two grounds being the furthest apart in the Championship.

QUEENS PARK RANGERS
GROUND: Loftus Road **CAPACITY:** 18,193
MANAGER: Martí Cifuentes **NICKNAME:** The Hoops
2023/24 LEAGUE POSITION: 18th
DID YOU KNOW:
When Rangers sold Eberechi Eze to Crystal Palace in 2020, the £19.5M they received set a new club record transfer fee received.

PORTSMOUTH
GROUND: Fratton Park **CAPACITY:** 20,620
MANAGER: John Mousinho **NICKNAME:** Pompey
2023/24 LEAGUE POSITION: League One Champions
DID YOU KNOW:
Portsmouth amassed 97 points while winning League One last season, they fell one point short of equalling a club record best of 98 points from 2002/03.

SHEFFIELD UNITED
GROUND: Bramall Lane **CAPACITY:** 31,884
MANAGER: Chris Wilder **NICKNAME:** The Blades
2023/24 LEAGUE POSITION: 20th Premier League
DID YOU KNOW:
Sheffield United have won the FA Cup four times but have never reached a League Cup final.

SHEFFIELD WEDNESDAY

GROUND: Hillsborough **CAPACITY:** 34,945
MANAGER: Danny Röhl **NICKNAME:** The Owls
2023/24 LEAGUE POSITION: 20th

DID YOU KNOW:
120 minutes of football had been played when Josh Windass netted a last-gasp extra-time winner to secure the Owls promotion in the 2022/23 League One Play-Off final at Wembley.

SWANSEA CITY

GROUND: Swansea.com Stadium **CAPACITY:** 20,996
MANAGER: Luke Williams **NICKNAME:** The Swans
2023/24 LEAGUE POSITION: 14th

DID YOU KNOW:
In the history of south Wales derby matches against rivals Cardiff City, the Swans have never suffered a league double against their arch enemy.

STOKE CITY

GROUND: Bet365 Stadium **CAPACITY:** 30,089
MANAGER: Steven Schumacher
NICKNAME: The Potters
2023/24 LEAGUE POSITION: 17th

DID YOU KNOW:
Stoke City reached their first FA Cup final in 2011 facing Manchester City in the showpiece Wembley final.

SUNDERLAND

GROUND: Stadium of Light **CAPACITY:** 48,095
MANAGER: Régis Le Bris **NICKNAME:** The Black Cats
2023/24 LEAGUE POSITION: 16th

DID YOU KNOW:
Whenever Sunderland play Norwich City they compete for the 'friendship in football' trophy. This dates back to excellent rapport between the two sets of supporters at the 1985 League Cup final.

WEST BROMWICH ALBION

GROUND: The Hawthorns **CAPACITY:** 26,668
MANAGER: Carlos Corberán **NICKNAME:** The Baggies
2023/24 LEAGUE POSITION: 5th

DID YOU KNOW:
Just nine goals in all competitions proved enough for Brandon Thomas-Asante to top the scoring charts at the Hawthorns in 2023/24.

Women's National League
WATFORD WOMEN

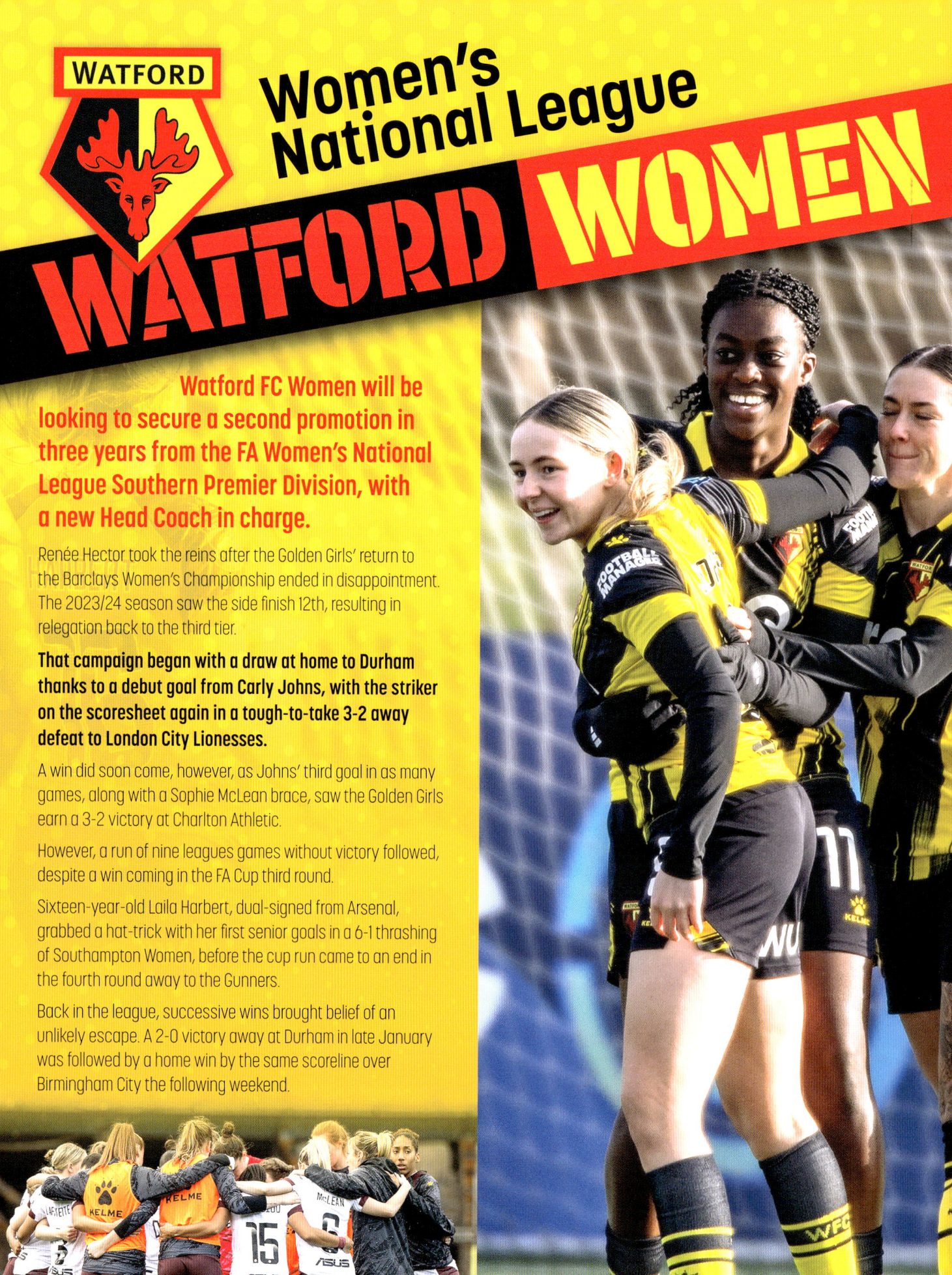

Watford FC Women will be looking to secure a second promotion in three years from the FA Women's National League Southern Premier Division, with a new Head Coach in charge.

Renée Hector took the reins after the Golden Girls' return to the Barclays Women's Championship ended in disappointment. The 2023/24 season saw the side finish 12th, resulting in relegation back to the third tier.

That campaign began with a draw at home to Durham thanks to a debut goal from Carly Johns, with the striker on the scoresheet again in a tough-to-take 3-2 away defeat to London City Lionesses.

A win did soon come, however, as Johns' third goal in as many games, along with a Sophie McLean brace, saw the Golden Girls earn a 3-2 victory at Charlton Athletic.

However, a run of nine leagues games without victory followed, despite a win coming in the FA Cup third round.

Sixteen-year-old Laila Harbert, dual-signed from Arsenal, grabbed a hat-trick with her first senior goals in a 6-1 thrashing of Southampton Women, before the cup run came to an end in the fourth round away to the Gunners.

Back in the league, successive wins brought belief of an unlikely escape. A 2-0 victory away at Durham in late January was followed by a home win by the same scoreline over Birmingham City the following weekend.

However, Watford could not build from the back-to-back successes. With Matt Bevans placed in interim charge following Damon Lathrope's move to the men's first-team, six straight defeats condemned the side to relegation with one game remaining.

The season did end with a 3-2 win over Reading at Vicarage Road, thanks in part to two Goal of the Season contenders from Coral Haines and Dré Georgiou.

In 2024/25, Watford are hoping for another successful third-tier campaign under new management, following promotion in 2022/23.

TOTAL LEGEND

POSITION: Forward
DOB: 01/02/1958
BORN: Falmouth, Jamaica
WATFORD GAMES: 503
WATFORD GOALS: 186

LUTHER BLISSETT

Prolific centre-forward Luther Blissett knows his place in Watford folklore is secure after a glittering career at Vicarage Road across three different spells.

The Jamaica-born forward currently holds the all-time club records for appearances and goals after finding the net 186 times in 503 matches as a Hornet. He was a major part of Watford's sensational rise through the leagues from the Fourth Division to the top-flight, playing under legendary boss Graham Taylor and always showing attacking grace and flair.

Blissett first progressed through the club's youth ranks and made his debut as a Golden Boy in the 1975/76 campaign. In the 1982/83 season, Blissett scored 27 goals to finish as the top scorer in the First Division, helping the Hornets to an outstanding second-place finish behind champions Liverpool just a year after being promoted.

His success in front of goal saw him become Watford's first senior England international, and in 1982 he hit a hat-trick on his Three Lions debut against Luxembourg.

Blissett briefly left Vicarage Road for a spell with Italian giants AC Milan but he was soon back in Watford for his second stint with the club from 1984 until 1988. He scored 21 times in his first season back in the First Division, and also helped his team reach the semi-finals of the FA Cup in 1987.

AFC Bournemouth was Blissett's next destination after he left Watford for the second time in 1988.

Steve Perryman brought him back to Hertfordshire for a further two-year spell in 1991, however, after which his playing career at Vicarage Road was brought to an end.

After retirement, Blissett later served under Taylor once more as part of the club's coaching staff.

He ended his international career with 14 caps for England, but it will be his club achievements in yellow - the promotions and all of the goals - which will be most fondly remembered.

WORD SEARCH

Words can go in any direction, even diagonals, and can overlap each other.

All of the Championship clubs' nicknames are hidden in the grid, except for one ...but can you work out which one?

```
Y H T O K D F Y E P M O P E W S V U Z L
D A E X B Z Z H K U C P I L G R I M S
N T F C S K Y B L U E S E X X O B G R O
E T I O M M P Q H S L E M G K X L T B M
H E Q D B C S T O W W B M L U T A J O G
T R B Y A L J I O T H H Z F O T C L S O
R S F K N P I G P W G I P D R J K W Y S
O T F H H V Z E S U W R T B O U C R Q Z
N S C O R X Z R A T S P N E B L A F N I
D L Z R B E V S A R Q C N D S Y T X G J
A W K N M S G S E E U V S Y Z Q S O E E
A O V E Z I T V D P O T T E R S M M Q M
P C Y T Z G O E H R I T S Y U N L S M J
Z O A S W R H A R H I B P M F W U K F Q
S A S N O I L F S A L B Y O A W O X S Z
N V O X A S D N T A L P E D W R F S R H
J Y R M W R I H D V U C W U Y I K F R G
U S E A A B I E K L R B D Q L F N Y K S
B L N N O C S E U D X K Q H E B T O J J
I S Q R Z D Q N S Q J N E F I D X W Y Z
```

BLACK CATS	CLARETS	NORTH END	RAMS	TIGERS
BLADES	HATTERS	OWLS	ROBINS	US
BLUEBIRDS	HOOPS	PILGRIMS	ROVERS	WHITES
BORO	HORNETS	POMPEY	SKY BLUES	
CANARIES	LIONS	POTTERS	SWANS	

ANSWERS ON PAGE 62

Watch out for these Danger Men when the Hornets meet their Championship rivals...

Danger Men

BLACKBURN ROVERS
Arnór Sigurðsson

Icelandic international midfielder Arnór Sigurðsson made a positive impression at Ewood Park during his debut season with Blackburn Rovers and great things are expected again from the 25-year-old in 2024/25.

Recruited from CSKA Moscow, Sigurðsson marked his Rovers debut with a goal against Ipswich, before then scoring on his home debut as Rovers knocked Cardiff City out of the Carabao Cup. A midfielder with a real appetite for goals, he scored seven goals from 20 starts last season.

CARDIFF CITY
Chris Willock

Cardiff City boosted their attacking options for the new Championship season when they secured the services of former England U20 international Chris Willock from Queens Park Rangers.

A potential match winner on his day, Willock can operate in several attacking roles, but appears at his most threatening when cutting in from wide areas.

After almost 150 appearances for Queens Park Rangers, Willock is Championship-smart and is sure to hit the ground running in south Wales.

BRISTOL CITY
Sinclair Armstrong

A summer signing from QPR, Republic of Ireland full international Sinclair Armstrong looks all set to provide additional pace and power to the Bristol City attack this season.

Armstrong's talent and physical attributes have seen comparisons drawn with former England striker Emile Heskey. Robins' boss Liam Manning appears keen to utilise Armstrong as the focal point of his team's attack.

COVENTRY CITY
Haji Wright

American international striker Haji Wright fell just one goal short of the magic 20 mark in all competitions during his debut campaign with the Sky Blues last season.

The powerful 26-year-old weighed in with 16 Championship goals plus a further three in Coventry's sensational run to the FA Cup semi-final. Forming an excellent strike partnership with Ellis Sims, Wright is sure to be one of the Championship's most feared forwards in 2024/25.

BURNLEY
Lyle Foster

South African international forward Lyle Foster appears set to have a big part to play in Burnley's 2024/25 season as the club bid to bounce back to the Premier League.

The 24-year-old forward was handed a starting berth in each of the Clarets' first three league games of the season by new boss Scott Parker. Foster netted five goals at Premier League level last season and will certainly be a major threat to Championship defences this time around.

DERBY COUNTY
James Collins

Much-travelled striker James Collins topped the Rams' scoring charts in 2023/24 with 14 League One goals as Paul Warne's men won promotion to the Championship as runners-up.

A full Republic of Ireland international, Collins was handed a new one-year contract at Pride Park in the summer and the 33-year-old will be keen to add to his Derby County scoring tally in 2024/25 and help the Rams establish themselves back in the second tier.

HULL CITY
Regan Slater

An industrious player in the Hull City midfield, 25-year-old Regan Slater can operate in a central role or in a wider position.

With an impressive range of passing skills and quick thinking in possession, Slater can often be the man to help the Tigers swiftly convert defence into attack. A League One title winner with the club while on loan in 2020/21, Slater is now closing in on 150 appearances in amber and black having made a permanent move from Sheffield United in January 2020.

MIDDLESBROUGH
Emmanuel Latte Lath

The Riverside faithful will be expecting great things from Ivorian striker Emmanuel Latte Lath in 2024/25 after the Middlesbrough man ended the previous season in a rich vein of goalscoring form.

After joining Boro from Atalanta in the summer of 2023, the impressive 25-year-old forward provided Michael Carrick's team with a true goal threat in the second half of last season when he netted eleven goals in the final three months of Boro's Championship campaign.

LEEDS UNITED
Dan James

Speedy Wales winger Dan James will certainly be the man that Leeds United look to for goals and assists as the Elland Road club aim to go one better than last season.

Few Championship defenders will fancy their chances in any kind of race against the jet-heeled 26-year-old who has the pace to worry any team. Last season saw the former Manchester United man score 13 Championship goals as he ended the campaign as Leeds' joint second highest scorer.

MILLWALL
Romain Esse

Teenage sensation Romain Esse appears very much to be the jewel in the Millwall crown right now having emerged from the Lions' academy set-up to start at first-team level.

Esse enjoyed an impressive 2023/24 campaign and after starting the new season with two goals in his first three outings, Millwall were swift to reward their young prospect with a new long-term contract. The England youth international is an exciting forward player who will certainly be one of the first names on Lions boss Neil Harris' team sheet this season.

LUTON TOWN
Carlton Morris

Carlton Morris netted eleven goals at Premier League level last season as Luton Town battled bravely to avoid the drop.

A muscular centre forward who is blessed with an immaculate first touch and killer instinct, the Hatters certainly see Morris as the man who can fire the goals to ensure an immediate Premier League return.

Morris netted 20 Championship goals in the Hatters' 2022/23 success and will be widely expected to do likewise this season.

NORWICH CITY
Borja Sainz

Skilful Spaniard Borja Sainz certainly appears to be the man that opposing defenders will look to keep close tabs on when facing the Canaries this season.

The tricky 23-year-old creator was in fine form for Norwich City last season as the Carrow Road club secured a Play-Off place. Sainz chipped in with six Championship goals plus an FA Cup cracker against Liverpool at Anfield. Blessed with great close control and exquisite passing skills, Sainz is certainly Norwich's creative force.

Danger Men

Watch out for these Danger Men when the Hornets meet their Championship rivals...

OXFORD UNITED
Tyler Goodrham

A product of the Oxford United Academy, talented frontman Tyler Goodrham entered the U's history books when his debut in an EFL Trophy match against Crawley in November 2019 saw him become the club's youngest player at the age of 16 years and 98 days.

He marked his League One debut against Cambridge United in August 2022 with an injury-time winner and played a key role in last season's promotion from League One with eight goals.

PRESTON NORTH END
Will Keane

Now in his second spell at Deepdale, Republic of Ireland international Will Keane topped the Preston North End scoring charts with 13 goals last season.

An intelligent forward player with an eye for goal, Keane provides a threat both on the deck and in aerial duels too, as well as being able to link-up play in the final third.

A vastly experienced Championship performer, Keene will certainly be Preston's go to man for goals in 2024/25.

PLYMOUTH ARGYLE
Bali Mumba

Highly rated wing-back Bali Mumba saw his reputation continue to grow last season as he played an important role in Plymouth Argyle's successful battle against relegation in 2023/24.

After joining the Pilgrims permanently, following an impressive loan spell from Norwich City, Mumba's ability to influence the game at both ends of the pitch was there for all to see. The 23-year-old featured in all but three of Plymouth's Championship fixtures in 2023/24 and chipped in with three goals.

QUEENS PARK RANGERS
Michael Frey

Much-travelled former Switzerland under-21 international Michael Frey joined Queens Park Rangers in the January 2024 transfer window from Belgian club Royal Antwerp.

A powerful 6ft 2ins forward, Frey marked his home debut for the Hoops with a goal to salvage a point from a 2-2 draw with Play-Off chasing Norwich City in February 2024. He began 2024/25 in fine form with August goals in Rangers' Championship and Carabao Cup campaigns.

PORTSMOUTH
Callum Lang

Portsmouth forward Callum Lang certainly put a marker down for what to expect from him in 2024/25 as he bagged an opening-day brace in Pompey's thrilling 3-3 Championship draw with Leeds United at Elland Road.

The 25-year-old joined Portsmouth in January 2024 from Wigan Athletic and netted a debut goal against Oxford United before adding another three goals in 12 games to help John Mousinho's side press on and win the League One title last season.

SHEFFIELD UNITED
Kieffer Moore

Having helped Ipswich Town to promotion while on loan from AFC Bournemouth last season, giant striker Kieffer Moore will be hopeful of spearheading the Blades' 2024/25 promotion bid following his summer switch from the Cherries.

The Wales international striker is a proven goalscorer at Championship level and his experience could prove to be a vital ingredient for Chris Wilder's side. Standing at 6ft 5ins, Moore will certainly be a hot favourite in most aerial battles.

SHEFFIELD WEDNESDAY
Josh Windass

Among the many new faces to arrive at Hillsborough in the summer of 2024, it was the retention of forward Josh Windass that may yet prove to be the Owls' best piece of business.

The Owls' goalscoring hero at Wembley in the 2023 League One Play-Off final, Windass was on target in Wednesday's final three games of last season as Danny Röhl's men pulled off a great escape to retain their second-tier status for 2024/25.

SWANSEA CITY
Liam Cullen

Wales international Liam Cullen certainly remains the one to watch at the Swansea.com Stadium.

The 25-year-old attacker popped up with another seven Championship goals last season - one of which set the Swans on the road to victory over arch-rivals Cardiff City in the south Wales derby in March 2024.

Having progressed through the club's youth system, Cullen is more than familiar with the passing game that head coach Luke Williams is looking to implement at Swansea.

STOKE CITY
Bae Junho

South Korean forward Bae Junho won the Stoke City Player of the Year award in his debut season with the Potters in 2023/24 and great things are anticipated from the 20-year-old again this season.

Blessed with great speed and an unpredictability that defenders find hard to fathom, Junho has the ability to weave forward and carry the ball into dangerous areas while getting supporters up and off their seats. He's certainly going to be one to watch in 2024/25.

WATFORD
Daniel Jebbison

Aged 17 years and 309 days, Daniel Jebbison became the youngest player in Premier League history to score on his first start in the division for Sheffield United against Everton back in May 2021.

Standing 6ft 3in tall, Jebbison is good in the air and supremely gifted with the ball at his feet. His speed and movement, and the ability to finish first time, makes him the kind of opponent you can't take your eyes off for a second. After three goals and two assists in 35 appearances for the Blades he moved to Premier League AFC Bournemouth in the summer of 2024 and was loaned to Watford for the 2024/25 season. He his most definitely one to watch.

SUNDERLAND
Chris Rigg

Teenage sensation Chris Rigg enjoyed a real breakthrough season at Sunderland in 2023/24 as he marked his Black Cats' league debut with a goal in the 5-0 demolition of Southampton at Stadium of Light in September 2023.

The 17-year-old went on to make a further 20 Championship appearances in Sunderland colours last season and could well be a regular starter and star performer under the club's new head coach Régis Le Bris over the coming months.

WEST BROMWICH ALBION
John Swift

A classy Championship midfield operator, John Swift contributed nine goals to the West Bromwich Albion cause in 2023/24 as the Baggies reached the Play-Offs with a fifth-place finish.

The 29-year-old former Reading man continues to display an impressive range of passing skills and tends to set the tempo in Albion games. Swift will certainly be one of the first names on the Baggies' team sheet and will have a key part to play at The Hawthorns this season.

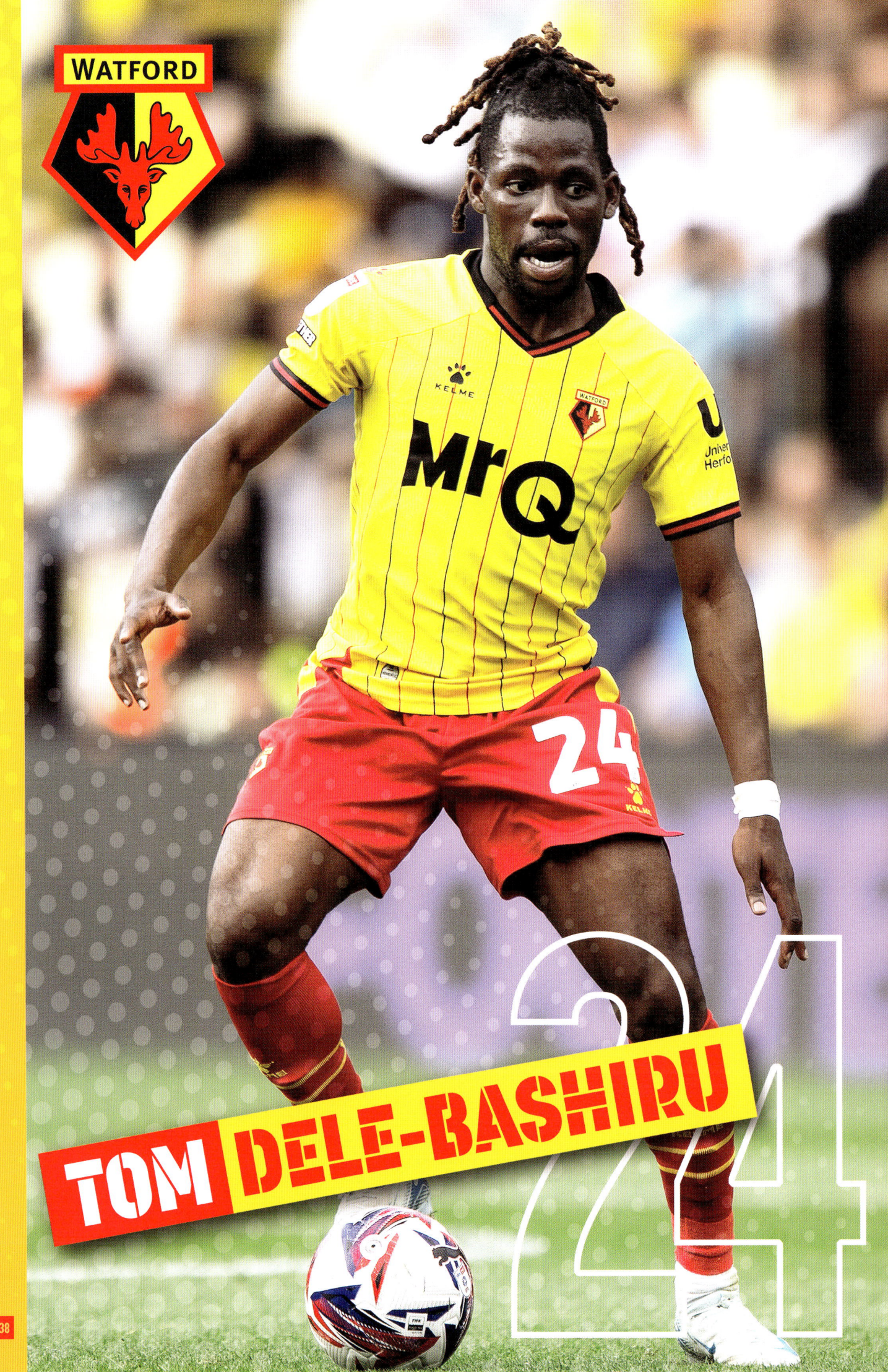

Wesley Hoedt joined the list of famous names who have had the honour of winning the Graham Taylor Player of the Season award, as voted for by Watford supporters.

23/24 PLAYER OF THE SEASON

The Dutch centre-back excelled during 2023/24 with a number of commanding displays in the Hornets' back four, in what was his first full season at Vicarage Road since his switch from Belgian club Anderlecht in January 2023.

Hoedt made it his ambition to play every minute of the season for the Golden Boys and was on course to achieve this aim before his booking against Coventry City in March, which led to a suspension.

A left-footer, Hoedt regularly impressed with his vision to pick out teammates and his exceptional range of passing, as well as always providing leadership, crunching tackles and communication at the back.

He scored in the 3-2 defeat against Middlesbrough in September and grabbed his second of the season in the 2-1 victory at Hull City in December, more on which can be found elsewhere in this annual…

The club's on-field captain then rounded off his season with his third goal of the campaign on the final day, against Middlesbrough again in a 3-1 reverse.

The Graham Taylor Player of the Season award was presented to Hoedt by Head Coach Tom Cleverley following the last home game of the season against Sunderland in April.

"I have to thank the fans for voting."

Hoedt said after collecting the award.

"For me on a personal note it's really nice, it's an acknowledgment of what you've done all season."

HOEDT

YÁSER ASPRILLA

Colombian winger Yáser Asprilla was named as the Hornets' Young Player of the Season after a standout campaign.

The South American often dazzled with his pace, skills and trickery, as well as his natural ability to beat his man.

After one goal in his first full season with the Hornets, Asprilla kicked on with six in 2023/24, including the winners against Sheffield Wednesday and Norwich City.

In the away fixture with Norwich, Asprilla scored a spectacular goal from distance and he followed this up in his next game with a thumping winner against Rotherham United.

SET UP A SQUARE WITHIN SHOOTING DISTANCE OF YOUR GOAL. PLACE A KEEPER IN GOAL AND A DEFENDER INSIDE THE SQUARE. YOU AND THE REST OF YOUR MATES ARE ATTACKERS AND SHOULD START AT THE OTHER SIDE OF THE SQUARE FROM THE GOAL.

FOOTY DRILLS

ATTACK ATTACK

EASY

Dribble into the square, try to beat the defender and dribble out of the opposite side of the square. If you successfully dribble through the square without losing the ball, finish with a shot on goal! If you lose the ball to the defender or dribble out either side of the square, you must then switch places with the defender so that you are protecting the square and they become an attacker. The next player in line can go as soon as a shot on goal is taken or the defender has won the ball.

HARD

You can make the square bigger to make it easier for the attackers or make the square smaller to make it easier for the defenders.

EXPERT

You can make the square slightly larger and add a second defender so that the game becomes 2 v 1 and harder for the attacker. To make shooting harder, move the square further away from the goal and encourage a longer shot.

The purpose of this drill is to focus on dribbling to beat a defender and finishing with a shot on goal.

Remember to take turns being in goal so that everyone gets a chance to play all positions!

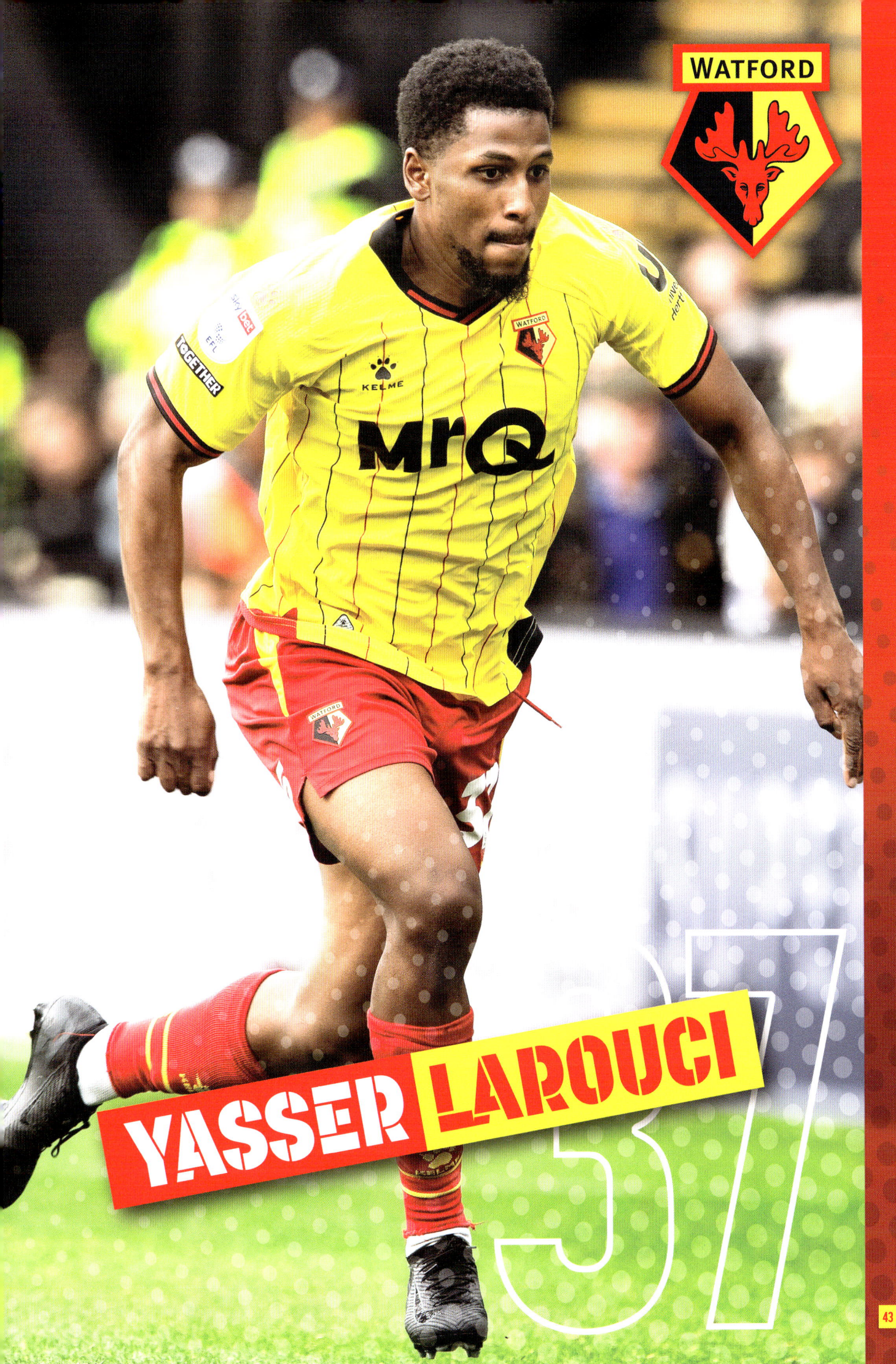

TOTAL LEGEND

It made perfect sense that Helen Ward's last act in a Watford shirt was lifting a trophy; raising the FA WNL Play-Off prize marked the end of a record-breaking career for the striker.

HELEN WARD

POSITION: Striker
DOB: 26/04/1986
BORN: Brent
WATFORD GAMES: 199
WATFORD GOALS: 161

A goal machine is an apt description; Ward was lively in the box, clinical in her finishing, as well as always managing to get on the right side of defenders with her runs in behind.

Ward's wonderful Watford achievements were meant to be; born in North London, she was raised a fan of the club before joining as a nine-year-old.

The Welsh international progressed through the ranks before making her senior debut as a teenager in 2001. This kick-started an eight-year spell with the club with Ward making, and scoring, on her international debut for Wales in 2008 during this time.

She departed the club in January 2009 to join Arsenal and completed two seasons with the side; her goals helping the Gunners win the title in both.

Further spells in the newly-formed Women's Super League followed with Chelsea and Reading, before she came back to Watford in 2017.

In her second spell with the club, Ward took her goal tally to 161, making her Watford FC Women's top goal scorer by some distance, and third in the club's all-time list.

This period included two promotions to the Championship, with the striker immortalised in a mural at Vicarage Road after hanging up her boots at the end of 2022/23.

Ward's international career was also a record-breaking one. Her 44 goals for Wales made her the country's all-time leading scorer until July 2024.

She has remained at Watford following her retirement, first in the role of General Manager for the 2023/24 campaign, before a move into the position of Head of Women's Football in July 2024.

FACT OR FIB?

Here are twenty fun footy Fact or Fib teasers for you to tackle! Good luck...

01 The Hornets are due to host the Blades on the final day of the 2024/25 Championship season.

02 New Burnley boss Scott Parker began his playing career with Charlton Athletic.

03 SAFC's new head coach Régis Le Bris is of Swiss nationality.

04 The 2024/25 season sees Oxford United competing at second tier level for the first time since 1998/99.

05 Watford last competed in the Premier League in 2021/22.

06 Of the 24 clubs competing in the 2024/25 Championship only five have ever played in the Premier League.

07 Luton Town's nickname is the Hatters.

08 Plymouth Argyle manager Wayne Rooney spent a month on loan at Preston NE during his playing career.

09 Watford defender Ryan Porteous is a full Scotland international.

10 Stoke City were last in the Premier League in 2016/17.

14 Blackburn Rovers are the only club in the Championship to have previously won the Premier League.

11 Sheffield Wednesday signed former England midfielder Nathaniel Chalobah from Chelsea ahead of the 2024/25 season.

15 Queens Park Rangers striker Žan Celar is a Slovakian international.

18 Bristol City signed striker Sinclair Armstrong from Millwall in the summer of 2024.

12 West Bromwich Albion signed 'keeper Joe Wildsmith from Championship rivals Derby County in July 2024.

16 Championship new boys Portsmouth play their home matches at Fratton Park.

19 Pompey forward Josh Murphy is the cousin of Newcastle United midfielder Jacob Murphy.

13 Mileta Rajović was Watford's leading League scorer with nine goals in 2023/24.

17 Watford re-signed former goalkeeper Jonathan Bond in July 2024 following his release from LA Galaxy.

20 Sunderland's Stadium of Light has the biggest capacity of all the 2024/25 Championship grounds.

ANSWERS ON PAGE 62

Wesley Hoedt needed to make space on his mantelpiece after the 2023/24 campaign.

23/24 GOAL OF THE SEASON

The defender made it an awards double in his first full campaign with Watford, collecting the Goal of the Season prize for his sensational effort away at Hull City, in addition to his Graham Taylor Player of the Season trophy.

The goal in question shocked every single one of the more than 20,000 spectators at the MKM Stadium that day.

It was a cold December afternoon on Humberside, with the game locked at 1-1. Momentum was beginning to swing in the Hornets' favour, thanks in part to Ben Hamer saving Jaden Philogene's second-half penalty. With 74 minutes on the clock, Hoedt ventured into the Hull half after noticing a loose pass into the feet of Liam Delap.

The striker's heavy touch allowed Hoedt to lunge in and win the ball, before noticing that keeper Ryan Allsop was off his line. He only had a split-second to make his decision, and that was all the Dutchman needed.

Pulling back his right leg in preparation like a wind-up car, Hoedt allowed the ball to slow in its roll before unleashing the might and power of his left leg to crash the ball towards goal. There was nothing Allsop could do.

The strike was so clean that the ball's end trajectory was decided the moment Hoedt sent it goalwards.

His marksman-like accuracy took the 40-yard distance out of the equation, lobbing the ball over the head of the 6' 2" shot-stopper before it landed perfectly into the back of the net.

WESLEY

The defender immediately sprinted to the opposite end, where the away fans were sat to lap up both their shock and appreciation for a winning goal that was worthy of earning victory in any fixture - the game ended 2-1.

Hoedt's finish was voted by Watford supporters as the best strike of the 2023/24 season, with his trophy presented on the pitch by Hornets legend Lloyd Doyley.

Yáser Asprilla finished second in the vote with his wonder-strike at Norwich City, while the first of Jake Livermore's two goals at QPR finished third.

HOEDT

TOTAL LEGEND

POSITION: Winger
DOB: 07/11/1963
BORN: Kingston, Jamaica
WATFORD GAMES: 296
WATFORD GOALS: 85

JOHN BARNES

England have a phone call to thank for discovering one of their greatest-ever footballers.

Bertie Mee, Graham Taylor's assistant, rang Ken Barnes to invite his son, John, to join Tom Walley for a youth-team training session after impressing his scouts playing for Sudbury Court. He accepted, and after scoring a volley in a match against Leyton Orient, John Barnes became a Watford player.

After impressing in the reserves, Barnes truly announced himself in his first start, away at Chelsea. Taylor said after the 3-1 win: "I think we may have unearthed a jewel."

Barnes played a key role in his first season as a professional despite only turning 18, as Watford earned promotion from the Second Division in 1981/82, completing their meteoric rise to the top-flight.

Despite his youth and inexperience, he made 42 First Division appearances, scoring ten league goals as he helped Watford to second. This remains the club's highest-ever finish. In 1983, Barnes made his England debut and he helped Watford progress to their first-ever FA Cup final the following year. Just a month after the final, Barnes scored arguably England's greatest goal.

Playing against Brazil at the Maracanã Stadium, he received the ball on the left before dribbling his way into the box, ball-rolling the keeper for good measure and slotting home for his first international strike.

Barnes continued to impress for the Hornets in the following three seasons, reaching double figures for goals in all competitions. The 1986/87 season proved to be his last as a Watford player. Taylor departed as manager in May 1987 and, not long after, Barnes made his move to Liverpool.

He went on to make more than 400 appearances for the Reds and, with Three Lions on his chest, the England man earned 79 caps and played at two World Cups.

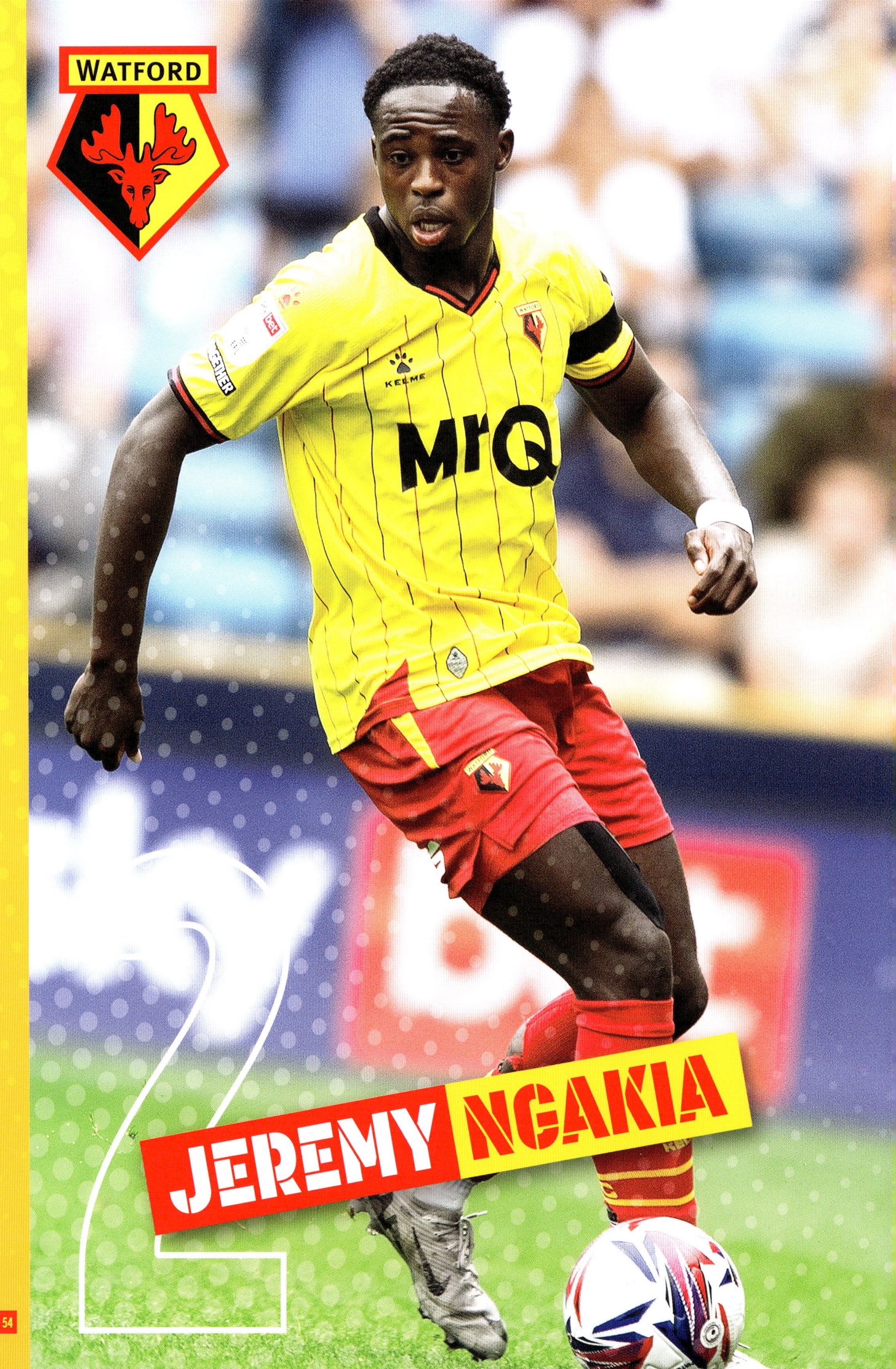

COMPLETE THE DRAWING OF THE CLUB BADGE

...and graffiti the wall with all things Watford!

SET UP THREE CONES IN A LARGE TRIANGLE. THESE BECOME OUR THREE GOALS!

MAKE SURE THE TRIANGLE IS BIG ENOUGH FOR THE GOALIE TO DIVE AROUND IN.

FOOTY DRILLS
SHOT STOPPING

The goalie stands in the centre of the triangle and three shooters stand opposite the three goals at their 'penalty spots'.

EASY
To start with, the shooters take it in turns to fire shots past the goalie. The goalie must work quickly to reposition himself for the next shot.

HARD
Players then start to fire shots more quickly. Just as the goalkeeper recovers from the last shot, the next player quickly shoots again.

EXPERT
Change the order in which the shooters take their shots. Shooters shout their names in any order, to signal that they are going to shoot. This keeps the goalie on his toes.

Also, be sure to try different shots. High, low, left foot, right foot, maybe even try chipping he ball over the keeper's head!

This drill is very tiring for the 'keeper. Remember to swap positions so that everyone gets the chance to be in goal.

TOTAL LEGEND

TROY DEENEY

POSITION: Striker
DOB: 29/06/1988
BORN: Birmingham
WATFORD GAMES: 419
WATFORD GOALS: 140

Troy Deeney was a trainee bricklayer after leaving school but the fact he eventually made his mark in football was very much to Watford's benefit.

The prolific, physical striker spent more than a decade at Vicarage Road between 2010 and 2021, enjoying two promotions to the Premier League in that time and a run to the FA Cup final. Deeney would end up playing 419 times for the Hornets in all competitions, scoring 140 times.

His last-gasp goal in the second leg of the Championship Play-Off semi-final against Leicester City in 2013 is one of the most dramatic ever scored, and certainly the most memorable at Vicarage Road.

After initially being used as a winger, Deeney found his feet at Watford in his preferred position as a striker. He finished the 2011/12 season as leading scorer and scored a memorable double against his boyhood club Birmingham City the following year.

Nothing could top the Leicester goal, however, which came deep into stoppage time with the tie level 2-2 on aggregate. Leicester were awarded a last-gasp penalty to progress to the final, but Anthony Knockaert's spot kick was saved by Manuel Almunia to kickstart a lightning counter-attack.

Jonathan Hogg's knockdown was emphatically finished by Deeney to send the Hornets to Wembley, while sparking a pitch invasion and scenes of delirium at The Vic.

The pictures of Deeney celebrating in the crowd with his shirt off will live long in the memory and, although the Hornets lost the final 1-0 to Crystal Palace, the striker was not to be denied his place in the Premier League.

Named as captain before the 2014/15 campaign, Deeney helped Watford earn promotion to the promised land as runners-up, in the process becoming the first player in club history to score 20 or more goals in three consecutive seasons.

Deeney would then score 47 goals in five Premier League campaigns, before helping the club back up at the first time of asking with a second-place finish in the 2020/21 Sky Bet Championship.

ANSWERS

PAGE 31: SPOT THE SEASON
1998/99

PAGE 32: WORDSEARCH
Baggies.

PAGE 39: SPOT THE SEASON
2005/06

PAGE 46: BIG MATCH - GOALSCORERS
A. Charles White - 88. B. John Barnes - 85. C. Tommy Barnett - 153.
D. Ross Jenkins - 142. E. Luther Blissett - 186. F. Cliff Holton - 105.
G. Maurice Cook - 81. H. Troy Deeney - 140.

PAGE 48: FACT OR FIB?
1. Fib (They are due to host Sheffield Wednesday on the final day of the season). 2. Fact. 3. Fib (He is French). 4. Fact. 5. Fact. 6. Fact. 7. Fact. 8. Fib (Rooney never played for Preston North End). 9. Fact. 10. Fib (Stoke were last in the Premier League in 2017/18). 11. Fib (Chalobah was signed from West Bromwich Albion). 12. Fact. 13. Fib (Rajović scored 10 Championship goals in 2023/24 not nine). 14. Fact. 15. Fib (He is a Slovenian international). 16. Fact. 17. Fact. 18. Fib (He was signed from QPR not Millwall). 19. Fib (Josh and Jacob are twin brothers not cousins). 20. Fact.

PAGE 53: BIG MATCH - APPEARANCES
A. Tommy Barnett - 442. B. Kenny Jackett - 428. C. Nigel Gibbs - 491.
D. Lloyd Doyley - 443. E. Arthur Woodward. F. Luther Blissett - 503.
G. Duncan Welbourne - 457. H. Gary Porter - 472.

PAGE 56: SPOT THE SEASON
2018/19

PAGE 61: SPOT THE SEASON
2020/21

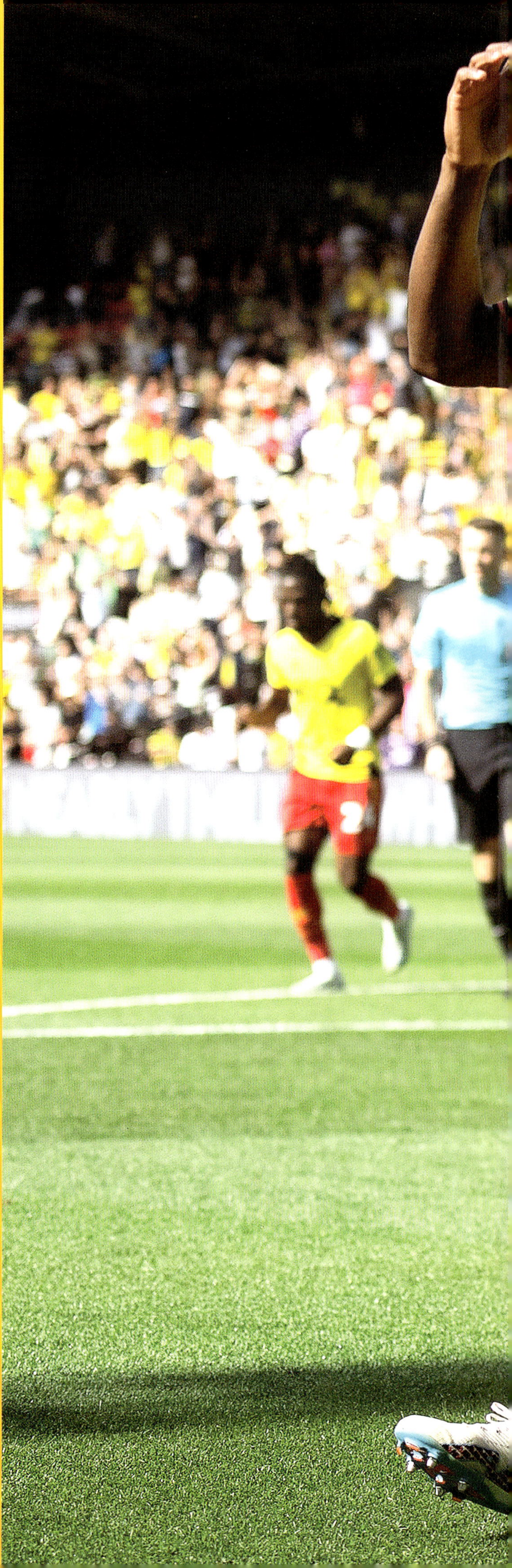